Ghost Story Mysteries

Solve It Yourself

Ghost Story Mysteries

Written by Carol Beach York
Illustrated by John Lawn

Watermill Press

Printed in the United States of America

ISBN 0-89375-693-8

Contents

All these stories are about ghosts. But are the ghosts real or imagined? That is a mystery *you* can solve. Read the stories carefully. Each one contains a clue that will help you decide if the ghost is real or not-so-real. Solve the mystery!

The Yellow House

Being lost on a lonely country road isn't exactly fun.

Ron and Dave didn't like it much.

They were driving home from college for a week of spring vacation. Somewhere along the way they had taken a wrong turn. Now every turn they took led to narrower, lonelier roads. And soon it would start to get dark. The last rays of the setting sun cast long shadows over the deserted countryside.

"How lucky can you get," said Ron. He slowed the car to a stop. It didn't matter if he stopped right in the middle of the road; there was no other traffic. The road they were on now was barely more than a dirt trail.

The last road-sign had said Turner Road. It sounded like a place where there would be a few houses—something. But so far there had been nothing but the slim, winding road, occasional patches of woods, and one old wooden bridge over a stream.

"What do you mean, how lucky can we get?"

Dave pushed back his cap and looked at Ron.

"I mean not only are we lost," Ron said wearily, "but we're almost out of gas."

Dave pulled his cap down over his eyes. "Wake me up when it's over."

"Very funny." Ron gazed around at the barren landscape. He didn't feel like making jokes.

"Okay." Dave came out from under his cap. "Why don't we go on a little further and stop at the first house we see. Maybe we can get some directions."

Ron stepped on the accelerator again, and the not-so-new car went on down the road. Dave's suggestion was as good as anything Ron could think of. The only thing wrong was that they hadn't seen a house for miles. Maybe there weren't any houses on Turner Road. And if they wanted to ask directions, they had to find a house first.

"My dad had a car once that could go for miles on an empty tank," Dave said hopefully.

"I'm not counting on that." Ron shook his head.

"That's what my mom always told my dad," Dave laughed. "She said she wasn't going anyplace with him in a car with an empty gas tank—but they always made it."

"I wish I had your dad here now," Ron muttered. "Or at least his car."

Suddenly, ahead in the fading sunlight, they

saw a house.

The house was set back from the road, and it would have been easy to miss. But the angle of the setting sun cast a brilliant, dazzling light upon the windows. It was a small, yellow house, and every window was blazing with golden light.

"Hey—there we go," Dave shouted, and Ron pulled off the road and drove up the narrow path to the side of the house.

The paint on the house was peeling in places. Whoever had painted the house yellow hadn't done it recently. But the boys didn't care about that. Like a miracle, here was a house at last. Surely somebody in the house could tell them the way back to the main road.

There was a small front porch on the yellow house. There were six steps leading up. When Ron and Dave walked up and stood on the porch, they were surprised to see that the door of the house was open a few inches.

Ron looked at Dave uncertainly.

"Go ahead and knock," Dave said with a shrug.

Ron knocked, and the door creaked open a few more inches.

No one came to answer the knock.

Ron knocked again.

"Anybody home?" Dave called boldly.

There was only the silence of the lonely countryside.

Dave stuck his head around the half-open door, and Ron pulled him back. "You can't go into somebody's house," he said.

But Dave pushed the door further open. "Anybody home?" he called again. "Hey, in there—anybody home?"

There was no answer.

"Okay, what do we do now?" Dave shoved his hands into the pockets of his jeans and looked at Ron.

"I don't know." Ron was disappointed. It was great luck to find a house. But if nobody was home, that wasn't such great luck.

Dave was waiting, and at last Ron said, "Why is the door open? Somebody must be home if the door's open, don't you think?"

"Beats me." Dave nudged the door with his foot, and the door opened further. It was all the way open now.

Through the open door they could see a hallway with a small table. There was a yellow vase on the table and a mirror on the wall above. But no sign of any people.

Ron and Dave looked at each other. They thought about all the wrong turns they had taken. They thought about how empty the gas tank was. They thought about how soon darkness would come.

This was the only house they had seen in a long

time. It was their only chance. They had to get directions from *somebody*.

Ron and Dave stood in the hallway uneasily. All their calls were met by silence. Deep silence.

On one side of the hall an archway led to a living room, but no one was there.

On the other side of the hall an archway led to a dining room. A long table was set with dinner plates and silverware. Two tall white candles stood beside a centerpiece of flowers. The tablecloth was lace. The dinner plates had gold rims. It was all very fancy and very beautiful.

And very empty.

"Where is everybody?" Ron whispered.

The house seemed to be completely deserted.

"I think we came to the wrong place," Dave said with a weak grin. "I don't think anybody's home."

He looked back along the hallway. "Maybe there's a phone around."

"Who are you going to call?" Ron stood in the archway to the dining room. The beautiful table stretched before him. Flowers, candles, gold-rimmed plates. But there was no food.

"Who would I call?" Dave spread his hands. "Anybody. I'll just say 'Help! Help!'"

"Very funny." Ron wasn't really listening. He was looking at the table. "Hey, Dave, look at this, look at the flowers. They've been here for a long time."

The bowl of flowers in the center of the table was wilted. Petals had fallen onto the lace cloth. Dried leaves curled up at the edges. It was the oldest, droopiest bouquet Ron had ever seen.

"Yeah, that's been there for awhile." Dave's good-natured face grew serious. He didn't like the eerie silence of the house. Why didn't someone come when they called?

Ron took a few steps into the dining room. He put a finger on a dinner plate, drawing a line across the film of dust.

"I don't think anybody's been here for a long time," he said slowly. "These plates are dusty. The flowers are dead." A bit of wax from one of the candles had melted onto the table. Dave poked it and saw his fingerprint appear.

All the rest of the house was the same. Silent, deserted, dusty. The furniture in the living room had an old-fashioned look. Two high-backed chairs were drawn up to an empty fireplace. A clock on the mantel had stopped, the hands pointing to nine o'clock of some past day.

In a little kitchen at the end of the hall the last rays of daylight glinted across a copper tea kettle on the cold stove. There was no food in the cupboard—just empty places where plates had

been taken out to put on the dining-room table.

Baffled, the boys went back to the front hall.

The light coming through the open door was fainter now. The sun had set. The yellow vase glimmered on the hall table. The mirror was dark.

"We might as well go," Ron said. "There isn't anybody here to help us. Whoever lived here must have gone away weeks ago."

"Maybe there isn't anybody here to help us, but *something* was here a lot more recently than weeks ago." Dave's face had grown pale. *"Something* was here just a few minutes before we came—and it's probably still here. We're getting out fast!"

"What do you mean—" Ron started to ask, but Dave grabbed his arm and pulled him out to the front porch.

Behind them, the open door swung shut with the sudden, vicious sound of a trap closing—just a moment too late.

The boys were safely outside. But what had Dave noticed that made him want to get out fast—that made him think they were not really alone in the empty house?

For the answer, turn to page 55.

The Ghost in the Lake

Karen and Julie heard about the ghost from Captain Swann.

They were sitting on the sandy shore of the lake early one morning, and he told them the story of the ghost. The girls hugged their knees up close to their chins and shivered. They had come out for a walk before breakfast, and the air was chilly. But mostly they shivered because Captain Swann's story was scary.

He wasn't a real captain. But he had an old sailboat and a captain's hat, and the people in the summer houses along the lake had nicknamed him "Captain." He looked like a sea captain with his white beard and sun-weathered face.

"Well," he began, staring off across the gray water under the gray sky, "this is just the kind of weather she'll be along. She likes the cold, misty weather."

"Who?" Karen and Julie looked around, but there was no one in sight. A solitary bird circled the water nearby, and waves lapped at the sand.

"I don't mean now." The captain shook his head. "She won't be along until dark. Late dark, round about midnight."

Karen's eyes widened with surprise. "Why would anybody want to walk around here at midnight? All the houses would be dark. Everybody would be asleep."

Captain Swann looked surprised himself. "You mean to say you girls haven't heard about our ghost? All these summers you've been coming up here? Well, well, that is a surprise."

"A ghost?" Julie hugged her knees tighter. She liked Captain Swann's stories, but he had never told one about a ghost.

"I don't know all the details," Captain Swann admitted, "but there was a woman drowned out there on the lake some years back. Seems she went out sailing one afternoon, and a storm came up sudden. The wind was high, and the rain lashed down so you couldn't see your hand in front of your face."

Karen and Julie stared at Captain Swann. They knew there was more to the story. He hadn't said anything about a ghost yet.

"Risky business, those sudden storms," Captain Swann said with a shake of his white head.

"What about the ghost?" Karen urged him to get on with the story.

"It's the ghost of that woman," the Captain said. "She likes the cold, misty weather. She walks along the shore, sort of pale and shimmery. Next thing you see, far out on the lake, is the boat she had. And that's kind of pale and shimmery too, like a ghost boat. She walks along the shore aways, and then—"

Captain Swann paused and Karen said, "What? What then?"

Captain Swann looked out across the lake. There was not even one sailboat in sight at this early hour. Only the vast, deep water under the dark morning sky.

"What happens then?" Karen persisted.

"Why then she walks right into the lake and disappears," Captain Swann said at last. "Then, after a bit, the boat disappears too—like she was aboard again, sailing it down to the bottom of the water. It's a sight to see."

"You've seen her?" Julie stared at Captain Swann with amazement. She had never known anyone who had seen a real ghost.

"I've seen her," the Captain nodded. "You can see her yourself if you come out here about midnight. She'll be along for sure, if this cold, misty weather lasts."

"Oh, I wouldn't do that." Julie shivered. The red sweater she had thrown over her shoulders wasn't warm enough to keep her from shivering at

ghost stories.

"I wouldn't be afraid," Karen said boldly. "I'd come."

Captain Swann stood up and dusted sand from his faded trousers. "Now don't rush into anything, girl. Seeing a ghost is something to think twice about. Some things are best left alone."

"But you saw her," Karen said.

"It was accidental." Captain Swann shook his head solemnly. "I couldn't sleep that night, and I came out for a breath of air. I wouldn't do it on purpose. I've heard that ghosts will take you right along with them if they've a mind to."

"Into the lake?" It was a long way from midnight, but Julie wanted to get up and run away right then and there. She didn't want a ghost taking her off into the deep, cold waters of the lake.

Even Karen was silent as Captain Swann said good-by and walked along the shore toward his little house by the pier. The beach seemed even more lonely now that he was gone.

"Do you think it's true?" Julie whispered, as they watched the Captain's figure growing smaller in the distance. "I bet he just made it up to scare us."

"Sure, he just made it up," Karen agreed.

But they weren't really sure.

"I'm going home to have breakfast," Julie said.

"Me, too," said Karen.

Neither one of them wanted to stay on the empty beach with the words of the ghost story echoing around them.

Julie's house was nearby, a summer house with a screened porch. Karen's house was further back through the trees. At Julie's front steps they stopped and Julie said, "I guess we'll never know for sure if there really is a ghost in the lake."

Right now, it seemed to her there were ghosts all around, lurking in the shadows, whispering with the lapping waves.

Karen hesitated a moment. Then she said, "There's one way to find out. We can get up at midnight and come down to the beach and find out for ourselves."

Julie was horrified. "Oh, Karen, I couldn't do that."

"Then I'll do it by myself," Karen declared.

"You wouldn't!" Julie's face was pale in the gloomy morning light.

"Yes I would—I will," Karen insisted.

Julie looked at Karen with awe. Karen was brave enough to face a ghost. But it might be dangerous. Captain Swann had said you should think twice about seeing a ghost.

"Don't do it," Julie begged. "Besides, your mother won't let you."

Karen tossed her head defiantly. "I won't tell

her. I won't tell anybody. And don't you tell anybody either."

"You'll fall asleep," Julie said hopefully. "You won't even know when it's midnight."

"I'll set my alarm clock," Karen said. "I'll go to bed with my clothes on. Then I'll get up at midnight and sneak down to the lake to see the ghost."

"Don't do it, Karen—" Julie begged again. But Karen turned to run along the path through the trees, toward her own house, saying, "I'm going to set my alarm for midnight right now."

"Karen—"

But Karen was already out of sight among the trees.

Julie's mother came out to the porch and opened the screen door.

"Did you have a nice walk?"

Julie gave one last look after Karen and then went up the porch steps slowly.

"Such a dreary morning," her mother said. And then she asked again, "Did you have a nice walk?"

"We saw Captain Swann," Julie said.

Her mother laughed. "Yes, I suppose he might be out early, funny old fellow."

"He told us there's a ghost that walks along the lake at midnight." Julie looked at her mother anxiously. "I think he made that up."

"I'm sure he did." Julie's mother laughed again. "He's quite a storyteller."

"He said she walks into the lake and disappears. And he said she might take somebody with her, if somebody was there."

"My goodness, what a dreadful fate." Julie's mother pretended to be frightened—but she was smiling at the same time. She didn't believe a word of the story.

Julie felt better, but still she wished Karen wouldn't go out to the shore at midnight—maybe Karen would change her mind.

But Karen didn't change her mind.

She was back at Julie's house right after breakfast.

"My alarm's all wound up and set for midnight," she told Julie proudly.

The day remained bleak and unseasonably chilly for mid-August. The sky was overcast. It was too cold to go swimming, and the hours dragged by.

"It's going to rain for sure," Julie's mother said.

But the rain didn't come until late at night. Julie heard it just before she fell asleep.

When she first went to bed she couldn't sleep. She lay awake a long time thinking about Captain Swann's story and about Karen going to the lake to see the ghost.

She thought about Karen, with her little bedside clock ticking ready to ring and wake her up at midnight.

And then as Julie drifted off to sleep, the rain began.

A late rain, with no one to see it but the ghost and Karen.

Even before breakfast the next morning, Julie started toward Karen's house. And there was Karen, safe and sound, coming along the path through the trees on her way to Julie's house.

"Did you go, did you go?" Julie plunged right in.

"Of course I went," Karen said. "I told you I would."

"Did you see the ghost?"

"Yes, I did." Karen lowered her voice and glanced around. But there was no one there to hear her except Julie.

"My alarm woke me up at midnight. I sneaked out of the house, and I went down and hid behind the big tree at the end of the path. I waited a few minutes, and then I saw the ghost."

"You went in the rain?" Julie asked with surprise.

"I didn't mind a little rain," Karen scoffed. "At first it was so dark and misty I thought I wouldn't see the ghost—but she was glowing with a funny kind of light, like Captain Swann said, so it was easy to see her. She was walking on the sand, all soft and glowing, and I saw the boat out on the lake—like a ghost boat."

Julie's eyes were as big as saucers. She didn't know what to expect next.

"And then," Karen said, "she walked into the lake and disappeared, just like Captain Swann said."

"She didn't take you with her?" Julie was barely breathing.

"She didn't see me," Karen shook her head, "or she would have taken me. I stayed behind the tree. Now I've seen a real ghost."

They walked back along the path toward Julie's house, and then past the house and down to the shore. The sand was cool and damp from the night's rain. Out on the water they could see the sail of Captain Swann's boat. He was out early.

Karen and Julie sat down on a rock in a little nook where a few scrubby bushes grew. They sat and looked out at the deep, dark lake where the ghost had gone.

After a bit Karen reached down and took up a handful of sand. She let it sift through her fingers in damp clumps.

"I was only kidding," she said. "I didn't really get up last night—I didn't really see a ghost."

Karen didn't want to admit she was afraid to go to the lake in the dark of night to see a ghost, so she had just pretended to be brave.

She'd made up a good story, but she had also made a mistake.

Julie didn't catch the mistake, or she would have known Karen didn't get up at midnight to see a ghost walk into the lake.

What was wrong with Karen's story?

For the answer, turn to page 55.

Trick-or-Treat

Nancy was going to be a gypsy for Halloween. She had a long red skirt, a pair of golden earrings, and six dime-store bracelets.

Tommy was going to be a skeleton. His costume was a shiny black suit with white bones on the front.

Jack wasn't going to be anything.

"I'm too old to go trick-or-treating," he said. "I'm going to stay home this year and watch television."

Tommy was surprised. "Don't you want any candy?"

"Maybe I can have some of yours," Jack teased.

Tommy thought about this. Then he said, "Sure, you can have some of my candy." His little face was solemn.

Nancy swished her long red skirt. She had put rouge on her cheeks and bright red polish on all her fingernails. It was fun being a gypsy. All her bracelets jangled and jingled when she moved her arm.

Their mother said, "Good-by, have a good time. You take care of Tommy, Nancy."

The front door closed behind the gypsy and the skeleton. They set off into the cool October evening with their trick-or-treat bags and a lot of jingling noise from Nancy.

They had not gone far before the ghost began to follow them.

Nancy saw the ghost first. But she wasn't quite sure what she saw. It looked like a dim, white figure coming out from behind a tree, then it disappeared behind another tree. It gave her a strange feeling. She took tighter hold of Tommy's hand, and they trudged up the steps of Mr. Brown's house.

"My, my, a gypsy queen and a graveyard skeleton," Mr. Brown greeted Nancy and Tommy cheerfully. Nancy giggled and jingled her jewelry. Tommy held out the shopping bag that was nearly as big as he was. "Trick-or-treat," he cried.

Mr. Brown dropped a candy bar into Tommy's bag and a candy bar into Nancy's bag.

"Thank you."

They went down the steps and out to the sidewalk again.

And there was the ghost, waiting at the side of the house. It came after them softly and silently—always just far enough behind so that

Nancy wasn't sure if it was there. She kept looking back over her shoulder.

"What's the matter?" Tommy tugged Nancy's hand.

"There's a ghost following us," Nancy whispered. Then she began to laugh. "It's Jack, I bet. He said he wasn't coming out to trick-or-treat, and now he's trying to scare us."

Tommy looked back at the tall white figure looming in the light of the streetlamp. It didn't look like Jack. Jack was always joking and teasing. The white-shrouded figure in the lamplight didn't look jolly, like Jack was. As Tommy watched, the figure moved away from the light and vanished into the darkness.

"How do you know it's Jack?" Tommy looked up at Nancy doubtfully.

"Who else could it be?" Nancy said. "Now come on—here's Mrs. Marten's house. Look, she's got a pumpkin in her window."

They went up the steps to a small porch, and Nancy rang the doorbell.

Before she opened the door, Mrs. Marten turned on the porch light. Nancy and Tommy stood flooded in light. Then Mrs. Marten opened the door and put a popcorn ball into each bag. Nice big popcorn balls, in clear plastic wrapping.

"Thank you," Nancy said politely.

Tommy said thank you, too, but as they went

back down the porch steps he told Nancy, "I'd rather have candy."

"*Sssh,*" Nancy said, "she'll hear."

But Mrs. Marten had already closed the front door.

The porch light clicked off.

And there was the ghost again, lurking near the bottom of the steps. It moved off into the darkness as Nancy and Tommy came along.

But it was there, somewhere close in the darkness. The gypsy and the skeleton knew it was there. "Are you sure it's Jack?" Tommy held tight to Nancy's hand.

"Well," Nancy said hopefully, "I'm pretty sure."

At the next house, Nancy and Tommy caught up with some other trick-or-treaters. They were clustered at Dr. Brennan's door. Candy was rattling into their bags in great handfuls. "There you are," Mrs. Brennan was saying as she dropped candy into the bags of a pirate, a red devil, and a bat-lady (who was really Nancy's friend Ellen McCormack in a black cape).

After that Nancy felt a little better. She and Tommy trooped along with the pirate and the devil and the bat-lady. It was good to have friendly company. The bat-lady's cape billowed around her magnificently. Nancy's gypsy bracelets jangled. The red devil tried to keep his tail out of

everybody's way. The trick-or-treat bags were filling up.

But always, just a short way behind, came the white ghost. Appearing. Disappearing. Appearing again.

Maybe it really wasn't Jack, Nancy thought. Jack would want to have a bag and get his share of candy, but the ghost never came to the doorways of the houses. She looked back again, and the ghost slipped out from behind a parked car and stood watching them.

The last house was the Dale house. Jeannie Dale came to the door. She was in college now, too grown-up to go trick-or-treating. Like Jack. Well, Jack wasn't exactly in college yet, but he was in high school. He thought he was too old to go trick-or-treating.

"Oh, you just scare me to death," Jeannie said when she saw the trick-or-treaters.

Nancy held out her red skirt and made a curtsey. She thought she looked very beautiful. She wasn't supposed to scare anybody to death.

But Jeannie Dale kept right on saying how scared she was.

"You all look so dreadful! What will I do!"

I don't look dreadful, Nancy thought. I'm a gypsy queen.

Candy fell into the trick-or-treat bags.

"Thank you."

Nancy and Tommy went down the steps of the Dale house. Their own house was just next door. They had been around three blocks gathering treats. Now it was time to go home.

The bat-lady and the pirate and the red devil with his long tail went on down the street, and Nancy and Tommy cut across the stubby, dried October grass of their front lawn.

The ghost was gone. Nancy looked over her shoulder, but the sidewalk was deserted. No white figure came out from behind a tree to scare her. Somehow the empty street was even spookier. Nancy was glad she was close to home.

"We sure got a lot of stuff!" Tommy ran ahead of Nancy to be the first to show their mother.

Nancy took one last look. The street was still empty. The ghost was gone. It *was* Jack, she told herself firmly, it *was*. And she was sure she was right when she came into the house. The living room was quiet. The television set wasn't on, and Jack wasn't there. No one was there.

Nancy could hear her mother's voice in the kitchen, and then Jack came strolling from the kitchen with a can of soda.

"How was the trick-or-treating?" he asked, flopping down on the couch by the windows.

"I thought you were going to watch television," Nancy said suspiciously.

"I did." Jack drank some of the soda. "I watched a Wolf Man and a Frankenstein movie."

"You didn't." Nancy set down her trick-or-treat bag with a thump. "You dressed up like a ghost and followed us—we saw you."

"A *what?*" Jack looked at Nancy in bewilderment.

"You followed us—I saw you," Nancy insisted.

"I told you, I stayed home and watched TV."

Jack looked very comfortable, relaxing on the couch. He looked like he had been home all evening.

"You can't fool me," Nancy said. But she didn't feel quite so sure now. Maybe it hadn't been Jack after all.

But then who had she seen on the dark street?

"We saw you," Tommy said—but he was more interested in candy. He was dumping the contents of his trick-or-treat bag into the middle of the floor. "Hey, Mom—" he started to call, but his mother was already coming from the kitchen.

"Look at that!" she said when she saw all Tommy's candy.

"Yeah, look at that." Jack set down his can of soda and knelt beside Tommy on the floor. "Look at all that candy!"

"You can have some," the little skeleton offered.

Jack took the popcorn ball. "Let's see how well Mrs. Marten can make popcorn balls."

Tommy shrugged. "I'd rather have candy," he said.

"I know." Nancy laughed. "You told me."

She turned to her mother. "Ellen was a bat-lady again."

And another Halloween was over.

Just before Nancy went to bed, Tommy came to the door of her room. In his pajamas he didn't look much like the fearful skeleton that had stalked the streets a short time before. His hair was damp at the edges, from when he washed his face. He looked very small.

"Was it really Jack?" he asked, standing close to Nancy.

"Yes, it was Jack." Nancy pushed back the damp, tousled hair. "It really was Jack. He was just teasing us."

How did Nancy know it really was Jack, dressed as a ghost, following them through the night?

For the answer, turn to page 56.

The Living Room

Ginny Baxter lived in the suburb of Greenfield. Her house was only a few blocks from the Greenfield Shopping Center. When summer vacation started, she walked over to the shopping center to see if she could get a summer job at one of the stores.

She got a job at *The Golden Page*, a big bookstore with fancy red carpeting and all the newest, most popular books. She was to start the very next day.

That was good news to tell her mother and father—but she came home with even bigger news than that.

First, she told her mother and father about the job. Then she said, "And look at the book I found at the bookstore!" Her eyes were shining with excitement.

"I thought you wanted to get away from books for the summer," her father teased.

Mrs. Baxter was looking at the book. The cover was black, with ghostly white forms that seemed to float across the blackness. *Haunted Houses* was the name of the book. By Arnold J. Westcott. On the inside flap of the paper cover it said that Arnold J. Westcott was an authority on ghosts and haunted houses. Each story in the book, each haunted house, had been thoroughly studied by Mr. Westcott himself. He had spent time in each haunted house.

"*Haunted Houses,*" Mrs. Baxter read the title aloud. "This *will* be fun to read."

She handed the book to Mr. Baxter, and he nodded with approval. "Well, well, somebody's written a whole book about haunted houses."

"But that's not all." Ginny had saved the best part for last. "Next week Mr. Westcott is coming to *The Golden Page* to autograph his books. I'll get to meet him!"

She paused a moment to let her mother and father realize what this would mean.

"Can I tell him about our house? Can I ask him to come and visit us?"

Mrs. Baxter smiled. "I don't see why not," she said. There was a touch of pride in her voice.

Mr. Baxter said he thought it was a fine idea. He thought it might be interesting to have their house written up in one of Mr. Westcott's books.

So it was settled. Ginny could tell Mr. Westcott about their house. She could ask him to come and visit.

Ginny thought the week would never pass. The days crawled by. She liked working at *The Golden Page*, but she could hardly wait for the day Mr. Westcott would come to autograph books.

Mr. Farley, who was the manager of *The Golden Page*, put a sign in the window announcing Mr. Westcott's visit to the store.

Arnold J. Westcott
Autographing copies of his best seller

HAUNTED HOUSES

June 26—12 noon - 2 o'clock

Around the sign Mr. Farley arranged copies of *Haunted Houses*. Then he went outside and looked at the window, rubbing his hands with satisfaction. The window looked very good, if he did say so himself. And on June 26, at two o'clock when Mr. Westcott finished autographing books, Mr. Farley was going to take him to lunch at the shopping center's best restaurant. The reservation was made. Yes, everything was taken care of.

On the morning of June 26, when *The Golden Page* opened at ten o'clock, a table was prepared for Mr. Westcott to sit at while he autographed his books.

All morning, as she brought extra copies of his book from the storeroom, Ginny kept rehearsing what she would say to Mr. Westcott. Ghostly forms floated on the black cover. A photograph of Mr. Westcott stared at her sternly from the back of the book.

Ginny wished he looked more friendly.

Mr. Westcott looked even more stern in person. His face was thin, and his expression was forbidding as he took his seat at the table, promptly at noon. Some customers were already waiting with copies of *Haunted Houses* they had just bought.

As the time passed, Ginny wondered when she would have a chance to speak to Mr. Westcott. When there was a lull in customers, Mr. Farley was always there, talking to Mr. Westcott, and Ginny felt bashful about interrupting. She really wanted to talk to Mr. Westcott alone.

But he was never alone.

At two o'clock Mr. Westcott stood up, looking around with the air of someone about to leave. To Ginny's relief, Mr. Farley was temporarily occupied on the telephone.

"Mr. Westcott," Ginny spoke his name timidly. She wished he looked more friendly.

Mr. Westcott smoothed the end of his neat, dark mustache.

"I wanted to tell you that I live in a haunted house. I mean, we have a ghost—you know, like you write about in your books. We thought—my mom and dad—that maybe you'd like to come to our house—maybe you could write about it."

Ginny had rehearsed what she would say, but it sounded jumbled. And Mr. Westcott, with his stern look, wasn't helping any.

"I mean—really—we do have a haunted house," Nancy added weakly.

Mr. Westcott regarded Ginny without interest. He saw a high school girl with long blonde hair and a freckled nose. All high school girls looked the same to him.

"And where might this haunted house be?" Mr. Westcott said "haunted house" with a mocking tone.

Ginny felt flustered. "It's near here—right here in Greenfield, just a few blocks away, on Elm Street—it wouldn't take you long."

Mr. Westcott did not look impressed. It was his experience that haunted houses were usually run-down old mansions with high ceilings and drafty rooms. Perhaps an occasional abandoned warehouse now and then. Or an isolated farmhouse with a family graveyard on the hill. He didn't think ghosts were to be found on quiet suburban streets. That was not the right atmosphere at all. Children playing, each house with its neat little lawn, garage, car in the driveway, bicycles propped by the front steps. No, that wasn't the right atmosphere for ghosts.

"It's not the whole house—it's mostly the living room," Ginny stumbled on with her story. "Sometimes we can hear noises in the attic or footsteps on the stairs. But mostly it's the living room that's haunted."

"Noises in the attic?" Arnold J. Westcott brushed Ginny's words aside with a flourish of his hand. "A tree branch rubbing on the roof. A frisky squirrel. Steps on the stairs? Houses make those little noises."

He glanced at his watch and started to turn away. He had not had lunch yet, and he was impatient to be on his way.

"But there's more." Ginny trailed after him. "In the living room there's a rocking chair that rocks. You can come into the room when no one's there and the rocking chair will be rocking all by itself."

Mr. Westcott turned back toward Ginny wearily. "Do you have a pet, young lady? A dog perhaps?"

"We have a dog," Ginny answered uncertainly. She didn't know what Taffy had to do with a ghost.

"Is your dog allowed to get up on the furniture? Lie on the sofa, or curl up in a chair?"

"No, he isn't." Ginny could see Mr. Farley hanging up the telephone. In a moment he would be coming over, hurrying Arnold J. Westcott out to lunch.

"Commonest 'ghost' of all." Mr. Westcott's thin lips parted with the trace of a cool smile. "I could retire a rich man, my dear, if I had a dollar for everyone who has told me about rocking chairs."

Ginny looked puzzled.

"Let me explain," Mr. Westcott said. "Pet isn't allowed on the chairs. Pet obeys. But only if there is someone to see it. But alone—" Mr. Westcott raised a finger dramatically, "alone, Pet has a nice rock for itself, or a nap on a soft rocker cushion. Pet hears footsteps. Pet jumps down from chair to avoid a scolding. Chair is empty but still rocking when Pet's owner comes into room."

Then Mr. Westcott was walking away again, and Ginny followed him helplessly.

"No, it's not that way at all—even when Taffy's asleep in the kitchen after supper, the chair rocks. And there's piano-playing in the living room—when we're all in the kitchen or upstairs. If you go toward the living room, the playing stops—"

"I'm afraid Mr. Westcott is running late." Mr. Farley was hovering at Ginny's side.

"Yes, I am." Mr. Westcott glared at his watch and mumbled, "Good afternoon, young lady."

Ginny's chance to talk to Mr. Westcott was over. She still hadn't told him the most important

thing, and now he was leaving.

Mr. Farley, wearing his best suit for the occasion, was opening the door of *The Golden Page*, whisking Mr. Westcott away to lunch.

"But Mr. Westcott, we don't—" Ginny didn't have a chance to finish the sentence. Mr. Westcott was gone.

She knew he would probably never be back to Greenfield.

Her house would never be written about in one of his books.

Mr. and Mrs. Baxter were as disappointed as Ginny that Arnold J. Westcott wasn't coming to visit their house.

They sat in the living room that night, listening to Ginny's story.

The living room was pleasant and cozy. A brown sofa stood against one wall. There were several comfortable chairs and the rocking chair that rocked when no one was sitting in it—at least no one the Baxters could see. There was a table with a lamp at each end of the sofa, and a table by the windows, where Mrs. Baxter kept her plants.

There was a large bookcase, with pretty pieces of china on the top.

There was a television set.

It was much like living rooms up and down the block, like living rooms all over Greenfield and the other nearby suburban towns.

Taffy lay on the floor by the bookcase. He was a very old dog, and he dozed off while Ginny was telling about Mr. Westcott. Taffy was the only one who really didn't care that Mr. Westcott wasn't coming.

"He wasn't very nice," Ginny explained. "He kept frowning and looking at his watch—and Mr. Farley was waiting to take him to lunch. I probably said everything all wrong."

Mr. Baxter shook his head thoughtfully. "It surprises me that he didn't show more interest. Ghosts and haunted houses are supposed to be his specialty."

"Just exactly what did you tell Mr. Westcott?" Ginny's mother asked. "It does seem strange he didn't show more interest."

"I told him about the noises in the attic, and the steps on the stairs. He said that wasn't anything—tree branches or something." Ginny shrugged. "I told him about the rocking chair and about the piano-playing. He made me so nervous. He was in such a hurry, and I had to tell him everything so fast."

Mr. Baxter laughed. "I bet you forgot to tell him the most important thing."

"I didn't forget," Ginny said. "I tried to tell him, but he wasn't listening anymore. He just left."

"That explains it," said Mrs. Baxter.

What had Ginny tried to tell Mr. Westcott?

What was the "most important thing" that would have changed his mind about visiting the haunted living room?

For the answer, turn to page 56.

Ghost Story

James Morey had seen sixty winters. Some were worse than others. But always there was too much snow. He hated it more every year.

He stood one evening at his front window watching the snow that had been falling steadily for several hours. Now the snow was stopping—only a few flakes fluttered through the darkness. All the sidewalks and yards and rooftops were covered. The street had a luminous white glow. Tomorrow the boy who lived down the block would come to shovel James Morey's walk. Snow meant money lost for James Morey. He closed the curtain with a frown and went to sit in a chair by the fire.

It was only eight o'clock, but he felt himself growing drowsy. He gazed into the bright, flickering flames, enjoying the warmth of the fire. His eyelids grew heavy...his head nodded...his eyes closed.

He didn't know how long he had been dozing when he was roused by a loud knock at the door. Still half asleep, he sat wondering if he really heard

a knock at his door. No one ever knocked at his door in the evening.

The knocking came again. There was a demanding sound to it, and James Morey left his chair by the fire to see what this nonsense could be.

A young man stood on the front step. "Hello, James," he said briskly. Then he stood smiling, as though James Morey should know who he was.

As James stared at this stranger, the young man laughed softly. "Don't you recognize me, James?"

There *was* something familiar about the face, now that James looked closer. A memory stirred in his mind—a long-ago memory. Yes, the face was familiar.

"Roger Loring," the young man said.

James stared with even more confusion than before. "Roger Loring?" he repeated the name slowly. The memory was coming back.

"It's been twenty years, but I thought you'd know me. Well now, aren't you going to invite me in?"

Without giving James a chance to say yes or no, the young man stepped through the open door and into the hallway.

James felt groggy from his nap. He didn't want company. He never invited company. And here was Roger Loring, the same Roger Loring he had not seen for so many years. In fact *exactly* the same, not a wrinkle or a gray hair. How could that be after twenty years?

The visitor gave James no time to figure this out. Before James could protest, the young man went into the living room. "Ah, here's a nice fire," he said, and seated himself in the green chair by the hearth.

James felt irritated and bewildered. His mind was full of questions, but he hardly knew which one to ask first.

"Surprised to see me?" The young man nodded with satisfaction. "I thought you would be. You should see the expression on your face."

"You—you haven't changed."

"Oh, that." Loring laughed. "I chose to appear as you knew me twenty years ago."

This was such a strange answer that James didn't know what to say.

"Sit down, relax." Roger Loring motioned to the other chair by the fire, the chair where James had been dozing. James sat down warily on the edge of the chair. He felt anything but relaxed.

The young man, on the other hand, was very much at ease. He sat back comfortably and took a slim gold cigarette case from his coat pocket.

"Cigarette?" He flipped open the case and offered it to James.

James shook his head impatiently. He didn't like the way Loring was sitting so calmly, as though he meant to stay all evening.

Loring lit a cigarette for himself and put the case on the table beside his chair. "Now if I could have an ashtray," he suggested in a pleasant voice.

"I don't have any ashtrays." James was becoming more and more annoyed with Loring's manner. What right had he to come barging in like this? Where had he been for twenty years—and why was he back now?

"You don't smoke?" Loring asked.

"No, I don't smoke."

"Don't you keep ashtrays for your visitors?" Loring shook his head with a disapproving smile.

"I don't have visitors," James answered

crossly.

"No visitors? That's a pity. Well, now you have me." There was an ominous sound to the words but he was still smiling pleasantly. "Well, never mind the ashtray. I'll use the fireplace."

The young man reached out casually and dusted the ash from his cigarette into the red flames of the fire. "This will do very well," he said.

"What do you want?" James demanded. "Why have you hunted me up after twenty years?"

Roger Loring tapped his cigarette. Ashes flicked down into the fire and were gone.

"I've come to haunt you, James."

"Haunt me?" James Morey leaned forward as though to hear better. "Did you say 'haunt'?"

Roger Loring laughed. "Yes, I said 'haunt.' Surely you've heard of ghosts haunting people."

James opened his mouth to answer, but the visitor waved his hand. "Let me explain," he offered with a gentle smile. "You cheated me in a business deal twenty years ago. I never forgot it. It took me five years to get back on my feet again. But I did, and I made up my mind that when the time came I'd get even."

"But—but—" James groped for words. "Why have you waited all this time?"

Loring's smile was not so pleasant now. There was a cold glint in his eye as he looked at James Morey. "I've only just now died," he said. "You

can't be a ghost and haunt someone when you're living. No, I've never heard of anything like that."

James stared blankly.

"You do remember cheating me, don't you?"

James couldn't deny this. He had cheated many people through the years. It hadn't helped much in the long run. He had never really gotten ahead.

As though he read James's thoughts, the young man let his gaze drift around the room. It was a tidy room, but the furniture was far from new, the carpet was worn thin in places.

"I've done very well myself." Loring's gaze came back to James.

It was easy to see that young Loring had done well. His clothes were expensive, the black coat trimmed with fur. The gold cigarette case was obviously a fine one.

And then as James stared at this elegant young man sitting in the chair by the fireplace, the figure seemed to fade a little. Through the body in the luxurious fur-trimmed coat, the back of the chair was visible. James rubbed his eyes. The firelight was playing tricks.

Even as James thought this, the visitor rose and tossed his cigarette into the fire. He stood a moment, looking at the things on the mantel above the fireplace. A clock, a china dog, a small brass bowl. Through the young man's body, James

Morey could see the flames of the fire.

"You may be wondering what it will be like to be haunted."

The firelight flickered through his fading presence.

"It will be hearing a soft step behind you on the stair. Feeling cold drafts of wind on hot summer days. A locked door opening and banging in the night. A whisper in your ear in an empty room."

The words hovered in the air.

A soft step on the stair... cold winds on hot summer days... a door banging in the night... a whisper in an empty room.

Roger Loring lifted his head and glanced about again. "You have a simple home, but I think I will be comfortable here. We will have long winter

51

evenings by the fire. You will never be alone."

The figure was fading more and more. Now it was just a bare outline, too hard to see. Through this outline the flames of the fire were strong and bright.

The figure faded and was gone.

Only the bright flames remained. James felt hypnotized by the shadows of the flames upon the sides of the hearth. The room was silent now. There was only the ticking of the clock and the crackling of the fire. The warmth of the fire was making James sleepy again. His eyelids were heavy...his head nodded...his eyes closed.

When James Morey woke it was early morning. He had slept all night in the chair, and he felt stiff and uncomfortable.

The fire had died out.

There was a chill in the room.

He sat for a moment, trying to become fully awake. He had never before fallen asleep and slept all night in a living-room chair.

At last he struggled up and drew open the curtains at the window. A pale dawn light glimmered across the snow that had fallen the night before. Every sidewalk and yard and rooftop was covered with snow. He had stood at the window, just like this, watching the snow stop.

Recollections of the evening just past swept over him. He had stood at the window and then he had gone to sit by the fire. He had dozed off. He had dreamed. Vague memories of the dream came back to him. The knock at the door. The elegant young man sitting in the chair by the fire.

Surely it was only a dream.

I've come to haunt you...a soft step on the stair...cold winds on hot summer days...a door banging in the night...a whisper in an empty room.

What a nightmare! James stared out at the bleak morning light. He rubbed his hands to warm them, but they didn't get warm. How terrible that would be, he thought. To never be alone again. To have always the unseen, unwanted presence of a ghost in his house.

But it was only a dream, he told himself. No one had really visited him last night. Look there, the snow on the walk was fresh, smooth. There were no footprints in the snow. No one had come.

But would a ghost leave footprints in the snow?

James Morey didn't know. The palms of his hands felt clammy. What if it wasn't a dream? What if it had really happened?

No, no, he thought with a sense of panic. It was a dream. It was only a dream.

At last he forced himself to turn from the window and look at the room behind him. The fireplace was cold and dark. The green chair was empty.

But as James Morey looked at this dreary room, he knew he had not been dreaming.

How did James know that he had not been dreaming?

For the answer, turn to page 56.

The Yellow House

The dinner plates on the table were dusty. The flowers were dead. But Dave knew that the two white candles had been recently lit when he touched the melted wax. Being able to leave his fingerprint in the wax meant it was still warm and soft, not hard the way it would be if the candle had melted a long time ago. When Dave realized this, he wanted to get out of the yellow house as fast as he could.

That night, the boys rode further along Turner Road. Luckily, they didn't run out of gas, and when they reached the end of Turner Road, they found a farmhouse.

An old man at the farmhouse gave them directions to the main highway. At first, the man didn't know what to make of their story. He said he had lived on Turner Road for fifty years and there was no yellow house on it. But then the man scratched his head and said, "Wait a minute, though. It seems to me when I was a boy, there was an old yellow house on Turner Road. But it couldn't be the same one you're talking about—it burned down more than forty years ago."

Ron and Dave found a gas station. They reached home at last and enjoyed their spring vacation.

But somewhere, in a house painted yellow, plates are set, candles are burning—and *something* is having a party.

The Ghost in the Lake

Captain Swann told the girls about the ghost early in the morning. When Karen came back to Julie's house after breakfast, still early morning, she said she had wound up her alarm clock and set it for midnight.

A wind-up alarm set in the morning for twelve o'clock will ring at twelve noon, not twelve midnight.

Karen didn't think about this, because she hadn't really set the clock.

Trick-or-Treat

Jack said he was going to stay home and watch television.

But when Tommy came back with his trick-or-treat bag, Jack said, "Let's see how well Mrs. Marten can make popcorn balls."

If Jack hadn't been at the foot of Mrs. Marten's front porch steps when Nancy and Tommy knocked at her door, he wouldn't have seen that it was Mrs. Marten who put popcorn balls into their trick-or-treat bags.

Jack had dressed up as a ghost to scare Nancy and Tommy. When they went to the last house, he hurried home, took off the white sheet, and came strolling from the kitchen as though he had been home all the time.

The Living Room

As you read the description of the Baxter living room, you will see that something is missing. What Ginny tried to tell Mr. Westcott was: "But we don't have a piano."

In the Baxter house, the sound of piano-playing came from a room where there was no piano.

Ghost Story

On the table by the green chair was a slim gold cigarette case.